# STORIES FROM
# PANCHATANTRA
## BOOK IV

RETOLD BY SHIVKUMAR

ILLUSTRATED BY PULAK BISWAS

Children's Book Trust, New Delhi

# CONTENTS

# THE BLUE JACKAL

Once a jackal was roaming about in search of food. It was an unlucky day for him. He could not get anything to eat.

Tired and hungry, he walked on and on for a long time. At last he found himself in the streets of a city.

He knew that it was not safe for a jackal to walk about in a city. But he was so hungry that he had to take the risk.

"I must find food," he said to himself, "but I hope I won't meet any danger from men or dogs."

Suddenly he heard the danger signal. The dogs were barking. He knew that they would soon be after him.

He was frightened and began to run. But the
dogs saw him and they ran after him.

The jackal ran faster and faster to get away from
the dogs, but the dogs were just behind him.

Suddenly the jackal ran into a house. The house
belonged to a dyer.

In the yard there was a large tub filled with

blue dye.  As the jackal ran, he fell into the tub.

The dogs could not find the jackal, so they went away.  The jackal stayed in the tub until he was sure that the dogs had gone away.  Then slowly he crawled out of the tub.

He was surprised to find that he had now become blue all over.

He did not know what to do.  He must get back to the jungle without being seen by men or dogs.

He quickly returned to the jungle. All the animals who saw him ran away in fear. They had never seen an animal of this colour.

The jackal saw that they were afraid of him.

He was quick to think of a plan to make use of this.

"Why do you run away?" he cried. "Come, come back to me. Hear what I have to say."

The animals stopped running. They stood at a distance and looked at him. They were still afraid to go near him.

"Come, all of you," cried the jackal again. "Call all your friends too. I have something important to tell you."

One by one the animals went to the blue jackal.

Tigers, elephants, monkeys, rabbits, deer, and many others, all went and stood around him.

"You need not fear me," said the blue jackal. "You are safe with me. God has sent me to be your king. I offer you all a king's protection."

The animals believed what he said. They bowed low before him.

"Your Majesty," they said, "we take you as our king. We thank God for sending you to us. Please tell us what you want us to do."

"You are to look after your king well," said the blue jackal. "You are to provide him with all the good food a king needs."

"Certainly, Your Majesty," the animals said, "we shall do everything for our king's comfort. What else can we do for you?"

"You must always be loyal to your king," the blue jackal replied. "Then the king will protect you from your enemies."

The animals were satisfied. They gave the blue jackal all kinds of delicious food and looked after him well.

The jackal lived like a king. Every day the animals paid their respects to him and told him of their problems.

The king listened to them and told them what to do.

One day, as the king sat in his court, a noise was heard in the distance.

It was the howling of a pack of jackals.

The blue jackal had not heard the voice of his people for a long time. He was lonely. Now he felt happy. His eyes filled with tears of joy.

Forgetting that he was now a king, the jackal lifted up his head and howled.

Immediately all the animals knew who he was.

He was only a cheap jackal. He had cheated them all. The animals were so angry that they rushed at him to tear him to pieces.

But the jackal was already on the run.

He ran and ran, faster and faster, and was thus able to save his life.

# THE BRAHMIN
# AND THE GOAT

One day a brahmin received a goat as a gift. He picked up the goat and set out for home, carrying it on his shoulders.

Three rogues saw the brahmin carrying the goat. They were hungry. They wished they could get the goat for a meal.

"That's a nice plump goat," said one of them.

"Yes," said another, "it would make a good meal for the three of us. But how can we get the goat? The brahmin will not give it to us."

"Listen," said the third rogue, "I have a plan."

The third rogue then whispered into the ears of the other two.

The other two rogues laughed. Then all three jumped up and hurried away.

The brahmin walked on.

Now one of the rogues suddenly came along and stood in front of the brahmin.

"Oh, holy sir," said the rogue very politely, "why

are you carrying that dog on your shoulders? Surely to a brahmin a dog is something unholy and unclean. I am surprised to see a brahmin carrying a dog."

"Dog?" shouted the brahmin. "What are you talking about? Are you blind? This is a goat I have just received as a gift."

"Now, don't be angry with me, sir," said the rogue in a calm voice. "I am only telling you what I see. But I'll say nothing more. Please pardon me, sir."

The rogue quickly went away.

The brahmin walked on, muttering angrily to himself.

A little further along the road the brahmin met the second rogue.

The second rogue looked at the goat and he looked at the brahmin.

"Oh, holy sir," said the second rogue in a sad voice, "you should not carry a dead calf on your shoulders. You know, it is disgraceful for a brahmin to carry a dead animal."

"Dead animal? Dead calf?" shouted the brahmin.

"What nonsense are you talking? Are you blind? Don't you know a live goat when you see one? This is a goat I have just received as a gift."

"Please don't get angry with me, sir," replied the second rogue in a very humble voice. "Carry a calf, if you want to, a dead one or a living one. It does not matter to me. I'll say no more. Please yourself."

On walked the brahmin. He felt a little worried. From time to time he glanced at the goat. It was a goat all right.

But very soon he met the third rogue.

"Pardon me, sir," said the third rogue, "but I must

tell you that what you are doing is most improper."

"Improper?" asked the brahmin. "What is improper?"

"It is not proper, sir, for a holy man to carry a donkey. A brahmin should not even touch such an unclean animal. You must know that yourself. Put it down, sir, before anyone else sees what you are doing."

The brahmin was now very puzzled. He was too worried to be angry. This was the third man he had met. And each one had seen his goat as something different. First a dog, then a dead calf, and now a donkey!

Was this goat, then, a goblin or some sort of demon?

Could it change itself every few minutes? Perhaps these men were right, after all.

Greatly frightened, the brahmin flung down the goat and ran home as fast as he could.

The rogue picked up the goat and hurried back to his friends. They were happy at the success of their plan. They had a good meal.

# A WISE
# OLD BIRD

Deep in the forest stood
a very tall tree. Its leafy
branches spread out like
strong arms.

This tree was the home
of a flock of wild geese.
They were safe there.

One of the geese was a
wise old bird.

One day this wise old bird noticed a small creeper growing at the foot of the tree. He spoke to the other birds about it.

"Do you see that creeper?" he said to them. "You must destroy it."

"Why must we destroy it?" asked the geese in surprise. "It is so small. What harm can it do?"

"My friends," replied the wise old bird, "that little creeper will soon grow. It will climb up and up on our tree and then it will become thick and strong."

"What of that?" asked the geese. "What harm can a creeper do to us?"

"Don't you see?" replied the wise old bird. "Some-one could climb up the tree by that creeper. A hunter

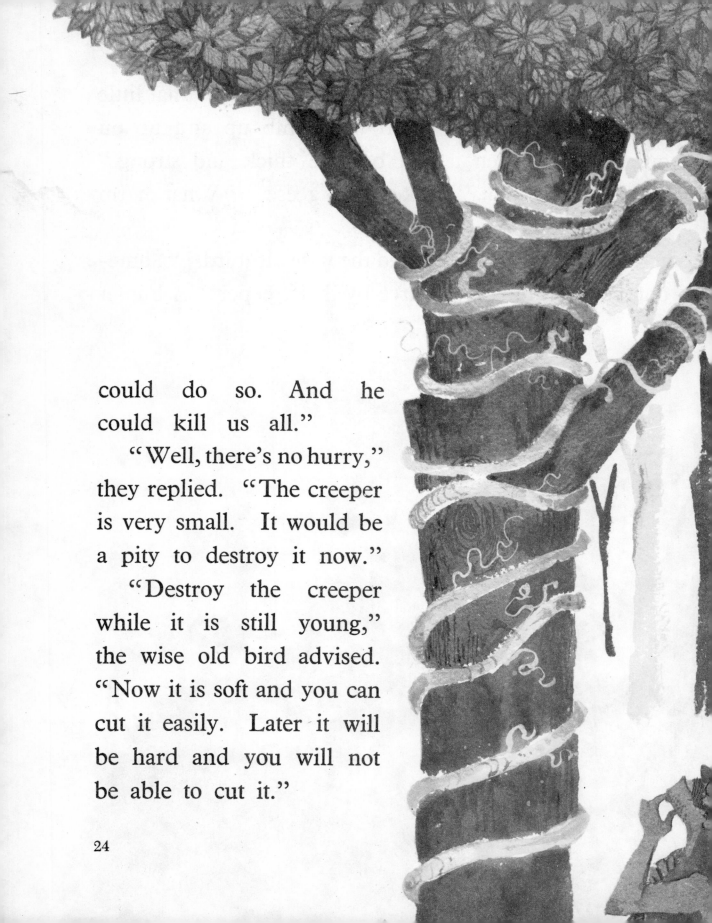

could do so. And he could kill us all."

"Well, there's no hurry," they replied. "The creeper is very small. It would be a pity to destroy it now."

"Destroy the creeper while it is still young," the wise old bird advised. "Now it is soft and you can cut it easily. Later it will be hard and you will not be able to cut it."

24

"We'll see. We'll see," answered the birds.

But the birds did not cut the creeper. They forgot the wise old bird's advice.

The creeper grew and grew. It began to climb up the tree.

As time passed, the creeper grew stronger and stronger. At last it was as strong as a stout rope.

One morning, when the flock of wild geese went out to search for food, a hunter went to their tree.

"So this is where the wild geese live," said the hunter to himself. "When they come home in the evening I shall catch them in my net."

The hunter climbed up the tree by the creeper. He

reached the top and there he spread his net. Then he climbed down and went away.

In the evening the geese returned home. They did not notice the hunter's net. As they flew into the tree they found that they were caught in the net. They struggled hard to get out, but could not.

"Help! Help!" cried the geese. "We are caught in the hunter's net. Oh, what shall we do?"

"Don't make such a fuss, now," said the wise old bird. "Long ago I told you to cut the creeper, but you did not. Now see what has happened.

Tomorrow morning the hunter will come back. He will climb up the tree by the creeper and kill us all."

"We were foolish," wept the birds. "We are sorry we did not listen to you. Please pardon us. Tell us what to do now to save our lives."

"Then listen carefully," replied the wise old bird. "I shall tell you what to do."

"Tell us, please tell us," cried all the geese.

"When the hunter comes in the morning," said the wise

old bird, "you must all pretend to be dead. Just lie quite still. The hunter will not do any harm to dead birds. He will throw us down to the ground to be collected and taken home. When the last bird is thrown down, all must rise up and fly away."

In the morning the hunter went to the tree. He climbed up the tree by the creeper. He looked at the geese in the net.

All the birds looked dead. The hunter took the birds out of the net one by one and threw them down to the ground.

The birds lay quite still until the last one reached the ground. Then all of a sudden they came to life. They rose up and flew away.

The hunter climbed down. He was very surprised at the way the birds had escaped.

# THE THIEF'S SACRIFICE

Long ago there were three young men. They were close friends.

One of the three friends was a prince, the youngest son of the king.

The second was the son of the king's minister.

And the third was the son of a rich merchant.

These three friends were always together. They did not take any interest in their studies. They did not care to do any work. They just spent their time enjoying themselves.

The king sent for his son.

"You are wasting your time," he said. "Mend your ways."

The minister sent for his son.

"I do not like the way you live," he said. "Mend your ways."

The merchant sent for his son.

"Mend your ways," he said. "If you don't, I shall turn you out of the house."

The three friends sat talking together.

"My father told me to mend my ways," said the prince.

"That is exactly what my father said to me," said the minister's son.

"And my father told me the same thing," said the son of the merchant. "He even said he would turn me out of the house if I did not mend my ways!"

"This is too bad," said the prince. "We cannot put up with such words from our fathers. Let us go away."

"But how can we go away?" asked the minister's son. "We have no money of our own. We have to get money from our fathers."

"Let us find a way of getting our own money," said
the merchant's son. "There is a mountain not far from
here. At the top of the mountain are precious stones
and gems."

"Let us go and climb the mountain, then," said
the prince. "If we find some precious stones or gems
we can live without seeking help from our fathers."

The three friends set out on their journey. They
crossed a wide river and passed through a dark forest.

At last they reached the mountain and climbed
to the top. They were in luck. Each one of them
found a gem of great value.

"Now we can go home," they said.

As they climbed down the mountain they thought of

the difficult journey ahead of them. Once more they would have to pass through the dark forest.

"There are robbers and thieves in the forest," said the merchant's son. "They might kill us and take away our gems."

"That is true," agreed the prince. "We must now think how we can get our gems safely home."

"I know what we can do," said the minister's son. "We can swallow our gems before we pass through the forest. We shall carry them safely in our stomachs."

"That is a good idea," agreed the prince. "No one will know they are there."

When they were near the forest they sat down to eat. Each one swallowed his gem with a mouthful of food.

It so happened that a thief was following the three friends. He heard what they said and he saw what they did.

The thief was happy. He planned to kill the three friends and get the gems for himself.

When the three friends were about to enter the forest, the thief went to them and said, "Good masters, ahead lies a dark forest. I am afraid to travel through it alone. May I therefore join you and travel with you?"

The three friends said he could travel with them.

They were glad to have one more man in their party.

Half way through the forest was a village. The headman of the village had a parrot.

He was very fond of his parrot. He could understand all his pet said. And he believed that the parrot always spoke the truth.

The four men reached the village. They passed the hut where the headman lived. As they went by, the parrot began to talk.

"The travellers have gems!" he cried. "The travellers have gems!"

The headman heard what his parrot said.

He wanted to get the gems for himself.

Quickly he sent his men to catch the travellers. The thief and the three friends were taken before the headman.

The headman searched them. But he could not find the gems. "My parrot must be wrong this time," he thought to himself.

He ordered his men to set the travellers free. The four then continued on their way.

As soon as they left the village, however, the parrot spoke again.

"The travellers have gems! The travellers have gems!" he cried.

"My parrot has never been wrong," the headman said. "The travellers must have gems with them."

Once more the thief and the three friends were caught and taken before the headman.

This time the headman made them take off all their clothes. But still he could not find the gems.

"My parrot always speaks the truth," he said. "The gems are nowhere to be seen. So perhaps you have swallowed them."

The thief and the three friends said nothing.

"Now I know what to do," the headman went on. "Tomorrow morning I shall cut open your stomachs. I shall get the gems all right."

The headman locked up the four travellers in a room, and put some men to watch them.

None of the four were able to sleep. All were filled

with fear. They could only think of the dreadful fate that awaited them in the morning.

The thief sat thinking.

"There is no gem in my stomach," he said to himself. "If I ask the headman to cut me open first he will not find any gem. Then he will think there are no gems with any of us. So he will let the others go free.

"In any case I have to die. So I might as well save the lives of these three young men."

The morning came. The headman was ready to cut open the stomachs of the four travellers.

The thief entreated the headman to hear him.

"I cannot bear to see the death of my dear brothers," he said. "Please be kind enough to cut open my stomach first."

The headman felt that he had no choice. So he agreed.

The thief's stomach was cut open. The headman found no gems inside.

"Alas!" he cried. "I have killed this man for nothing. My parrot has made a mistake."

The headman set free the three friends.

They continued their journey. Later, they sold their gems and became rich.

But they never forgot the thief who gave up his life to save theirs.

# THE GUEST

Once there was a bug. She had many sons and daughters, and they had sons and daughters of their own.

The bug and her large family lived all together in the corner of a huge and beautiful bed. It was the king's bed.

While the king was

asleep, the bug and her whole family drank his blood. They all lived very happily.

One day a mosquito flew into the room. He looked at the king's bed. He saw how soft it was.

"What a rich and comfortable bed!" he said to himself.

And the mosquito went to the bed. He stood there, enjoying the delicious perfume coming from the bed.

Along came the bug.

"Who are you?" said the bug to the mosquito. "Where have you come from? This is the king's bed. You can't stay here. Go away at once."

"Madam," replied the mosquito, "that is not the way to speak to a guest. I am a traveller, and in my travels I have tasted the blood of many people. Yet I have never tasted the blood of a king. It must be like honey. Now, as your guest, allow me to taste the king's blood."

"No," cried the bug, "you cannot."

"Why not?" asked the mosquito.

"Because," the bug explained, "when you bite the king you will hurt him. He will then jump up and kill us all. So please go away."

But the mosquito would not go away. He fell at the

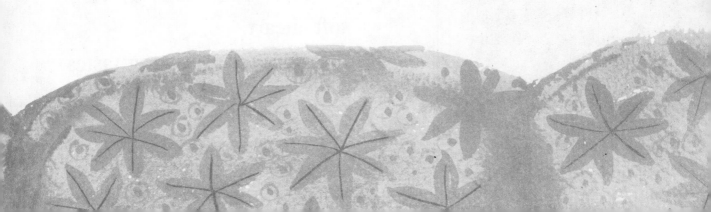

feet of the bug. "Please," he begged, "please let me stay to dinner, just this once. I only want to know what the king tastes like."

The bug had a very soft heart.

"It is true the king tastes very nice," she said.

"I will let you stay to dinner, just this once."

The mosquito was very happy.

"But remember," the bug said sternly, "you must not come to dinner at the wrong time, nor at the wrong place."

"Oh," said the mosquito, "then please tell me what to do. When is the right time? And which is the right place?"

"The right time," replied the bug, "is when the

king has eaten his dinner and drunk all his wine. He will then fall fast asleep."

"I see," said the mosquito.

"And the right place," the bug went on, "is the king's foot. If you bite him there when he is fast asleep, he will not know."

"Very well," agreed the mosquito, "I will be careful."

The bug went back to her corner of the bed.

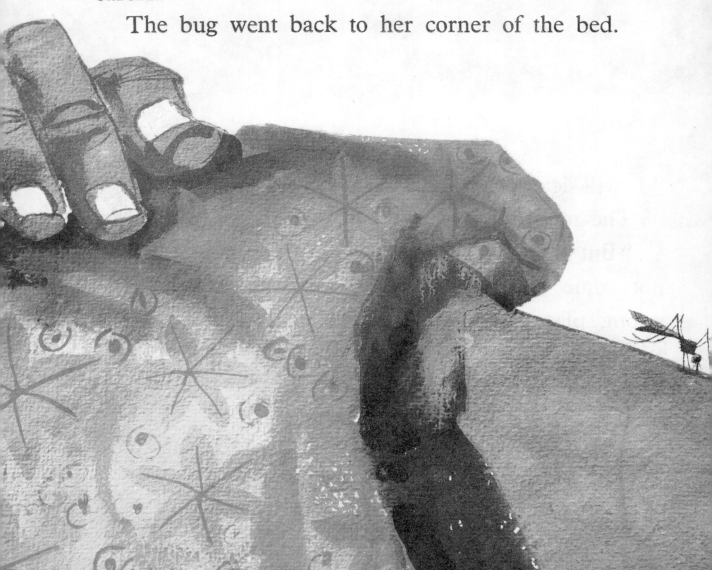

The mosquito sat and waited for the king to come.

As soon as the king got into bed, the mosquito became very excited.

"Ah!" he cried. "A king's blood for my dinner! It will be honey, honey!"

The mosquito forgot what the bug had said about the right time and the right place.

The king was just falling off to sleep.

The mosquito went and bit him in the neck.

Up jumped the king. He was very angry. He shouted for his servants.

"Come, all of you," he cried. "Something has bitten me. Hunt through the bed and find it and kill it."

The king's servants hunted through the bed. The mosquito had fled. They found only the bug and her family.

They killed the bug and all her sons and daughters and their sons and daughters.

None were left.

# THE LAKE OF THE MOON

A large herd of elephants once lived in a jungle. The king of the herd was a huge, majestic tusker. He looked after the herd with great love and care.

Once there was a drought in that place, for there had been no rain for a few years. All the rivers and tanks dried up.

Birds and animals were dying of thirst. Many of

them left the place in search of water.

The wild elephants also suffered much for want of water. The elephant king saw that if they did not get water soon many of his elephants would die of thirst. So he had to find water as soon as possible.

He called some of the clever ones among his elephants and sent them out in groups in different directions to find water.

Soon one group came back. They said that far away there was another jungle. In that jungle there was a large lake, full of water.

The king was happy. He called all the elephants and ordered them to go to the lake.

It was a large and beautiful lake surrounded by jungle. On the bank of the lake lived a large number of rabbits.

The elephants had to pass through this rabbit colony. As they went, thousands of rabbits were killed and thousands more were injured.

The rabbits were in a panic. Their king called a meeting.

"A herd of wild elephants passed through our

colony," he said. "They have killed or injured thousands and thousands of our fellows. We have to take immediate steps to prevent the elephants from killing any more of us. I want you all to think what we can do to save our race."

The rabbits started thinking, but none of them could think of a way to stop the elephants from passing that way again.

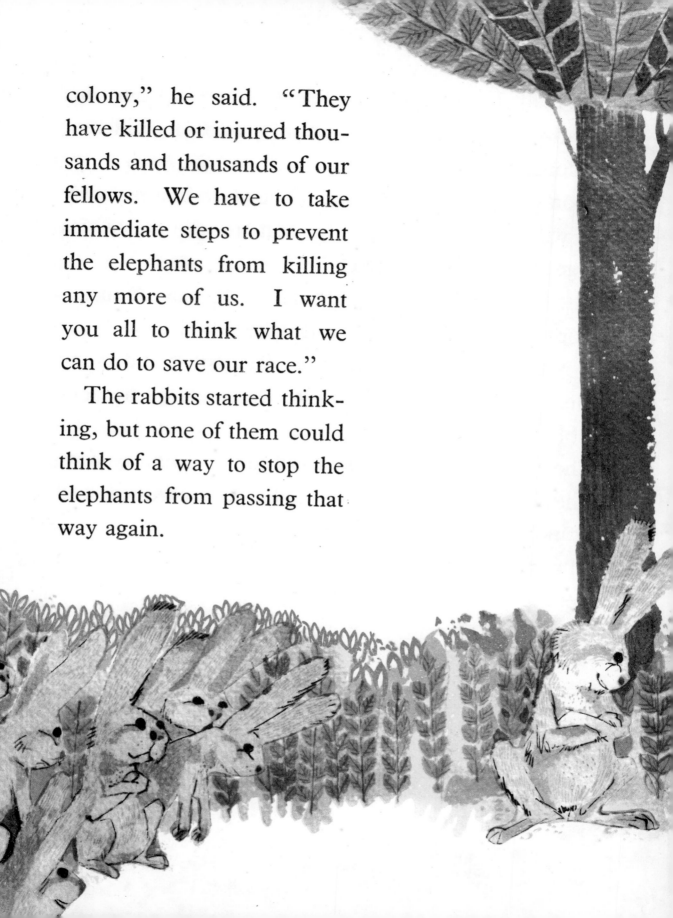

There was one little rabbit, quick and bright.

He stood up and said, "Your Majesty, if you will send me as your messenger to the elephant king I shall try to do something to save our lives."

"Very well," said the rabbit king. "Go by all means. Go as my messenger and see what you can do."

The little rabbit went out to meet the elephant king.

He saw the elephant king surrounded by huge elephants. They were walking proudly as they returned from the lake.

He feared that it would be difficult for him to get near the elephant king without being crushed to death by the crowd of elephants.

The little rabbit thought for a moment, and then suddenly he climbed up a tall rock.

"Oh, king of the elephants," he cried loudly, "hear me, please."

The elephant king heard him. He looked at the rabbit.

"Well, who are you, sir?" he said.

"I am a messenger," replied the rabbit.

"A messenger? From whom?" asked the elephant.

"I am a messenger from the mighty Moon," said the rabbit. "I serve the blessed Moon. It is the Moon who has sent me to you."

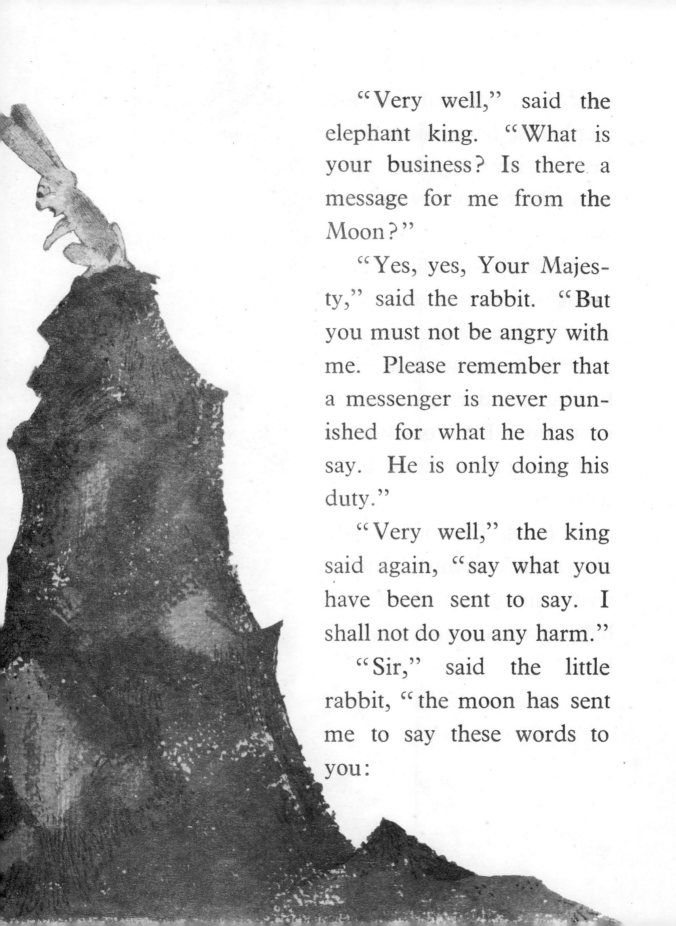

"Very well," said the elephant king. "What is your business? Is there a message for me from the Moon?"

"Yes, yes, Your Majesty," said the rabbit. "But you must not be angry with me. Please remember that a messenger is never punished for what he has to say. He is only doing his duty."

"Very well," the king said again, "say what you have been sent to say. I shall not do you any harm."

"Sir," said the little rabbit, "the moon has sent me to say these words to you:

"'You, the king of the elephants, have taken your herd to my holy lake and spoiled the purity of its water.

"'You have killed thousands of rabbits on your way to the lake.

"'You know that rabbits are under my special protection. Everyone knows that the rabbit king lives with me.

"'I ask you not to kill any more rabbits. Otherwise something terrible will happen to you and to your herd.'"